Winnie's MAGIC WAND

Korky Paul and Valerie Thomas

OXFORD
UNIVERSITY PRESS

Winnie the Witch jumped out of bed.
It was a special day.
It was the day of the Witches' Magic Show,
and Winnie was making a wonderful new spell.

She felt nervous.
'I hope nothing goes wrong,' she said.

Wilbur felt nervous too.
I expect something will go wrong,
he thought.

'What shall I wear?' said Winnie.
She got out her party dress.
Oh no! She had spilt red jelly on it!

Winnie threw the dress into the washing machine.
Then she threw in her towels, her pyjamas,
and her stripy tights.

She turned on the washing machine.
Swish, swish, clunk, it went.

When the washing machine had finished
going swish, swish, clunk, Winnie took out
the clothes and hung them on the line.

But her magic wand had been
washed as well.
Oh no!
'I hope it still works,' Winnie said.

Winnie dried the wand with a towel.

'I'll try it out,' she said. 'Something easy.
I'll change this apple into an orange.'

She closed her eyes, waved her wand, and shouted,

ABRACADABRA!

Suddenly there was an apple tree growing in her kitchen.
'Bother!' said Winnie. 'That wand's not working properly.'

Winnie dried the wand with her hair-drier .

'That's better,' she said. 'I'll try again.
I'll turn this apple tree back into an apple again.'
She picked up the wand, and shouted,

ABRACADABRA!

This time, the apple tree turned into an enormous apple pie.

'Oh no! **Oh no!**' Winnie moaned.
Now she really was worried.
It was nearly time for the Magic Show.
The wonderful new spell would be a disaster.

Wilbur was worried too.

Then Wilbur had an idea.
He ran out of the house,

MAGIC COFFEE MAGIC BOOKS MAGIC COMICS MAGIC FOOD MAGIC PETSHOP MAGIC CD-ROMS MAGIC FISH 'n'

... down the road,

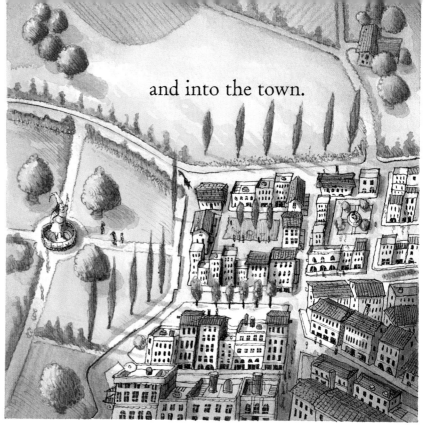 and into the town.

Perhaps *he* could find a new wand for Winnie.
He looked in all the shops.

But no magic wands.

Then, around the corner, he saw a little shop.
In the window was a big box of wands!

Wilbur grabbed one and galloped off home.

It was getting late.
Soon it would be too late for the Magic Show.
Winnie was very, very worried.

What could she do?

Then Wilbur ran through the cat flap with the new wand.

'Oh Wilbur!' cried Winnie. 'You are a clever cat.'

She didn't even have time to put on her party dress.
She jumped on her broomstick,
Wilbur jumped onto her shoulder,
and off they went.

They arrived just in time for Winnie's spell.
Everyone was sitting there, feeling excited.
Winnie always did something special.

'First,' announced Winnie, 'I will turn my
beautiful black cat into a green cat.'

She waved her wand, and shouted,

ABRACADABRA!

Wilbur waited . . .

Everyone waited . . .

Winnie tried again.

Nothing.

At last, a bunch of paper flowers popped out of the end of the trick wand.

One of the witches started to laugh.
Soon everyone was laughing.
They laughed, they screamed,
they shrieked and fell off their chairs.

'What a clever joke, Winnie,' they cried.
'Where *did* you get that wand?'
Winnie smiled.
But she didn't say anything.

And neither did Wilbur.

www.korkypaul.com

Winnie's Magic Wand is based on an idea e-mailed to Korky Paul by
Mr. John Fidler's Class Y2F, Akrotiri Primary School, Cyprus.

End papers by Ashley Richardson aged 10.
Thank you to Marcham Primary School for helping with the endpapers-K.P.

To Alexi K.P.
For Ron Heapy V.T.

OXFORD
UNIVERSITY PRESS

Great Clarendon Street, Oxford OX2 6DP

Oxford University Press is a department of the University of Oxford.
It furthers the University's objective of excellence in research, scholarship,
and education by publishing worldwide in

Oxford New York

Athens Auckland Bangkok Bogotá Buenos Aires Cape Town
Chennai Dar es Salaam Delhi Florence Hong Kong Istanbul
Karachi Kolkata Kuala Lumpur Madrid Melbourne Mexico City Mumbai
Nairobi Paris São Paulo Shanghai Singapore Taipei Tokyo Toronto Warsaw
with associated companies in Berlin Ibadan

Oxford is a registered trade mark of Oxford University Press
in the UK and in certain other countries

Text © Valerie Thomas 2002
Illustrations © Korky Paul 2002

The author and artist have asserted their moral right to be
known as the author and artist of the work.

First published 2002

British Library Cataloguing in Publication Data available

ISBN 0-19-279081-1

10 9 8 7 6 5 4 3 2

Printed in Europe